Text and illustrations copyright © 2009 Etienne Delessert

Published in 2009 by Creative Editions P.O. Box 227, Mankato, MN 56002 USA www.thecreativecompany.us

Creative Editions is an imprint of The Creative Company. Designed by Rita Marshall

Library of Congress Cataloging-in-Publication Data

Delessert, Etienne. Moon theater / illustrated and written by Etienne Delessert.

Summary: To prepare for the moon's nightly rising, a young stagehand performs such tasks as dressing the birds in long dark coats, training wild dogs to howl, and watering the stars.

ISBN 978-1-56846-208-0   [1. Moon—Fiction.] I. Title.   PZ7.D3832Mo 2009 [E]—dc22   2008053991

First edition   9 8 7 6 5 4 3 2 1

MOON THEATER

ETIENNE DELESSERT

CREATIVE EDITIONS

Every evening, the  moon

enters the wide stage of the night.

A very old man pulls the ◑ moon

up and sends it on its journey.

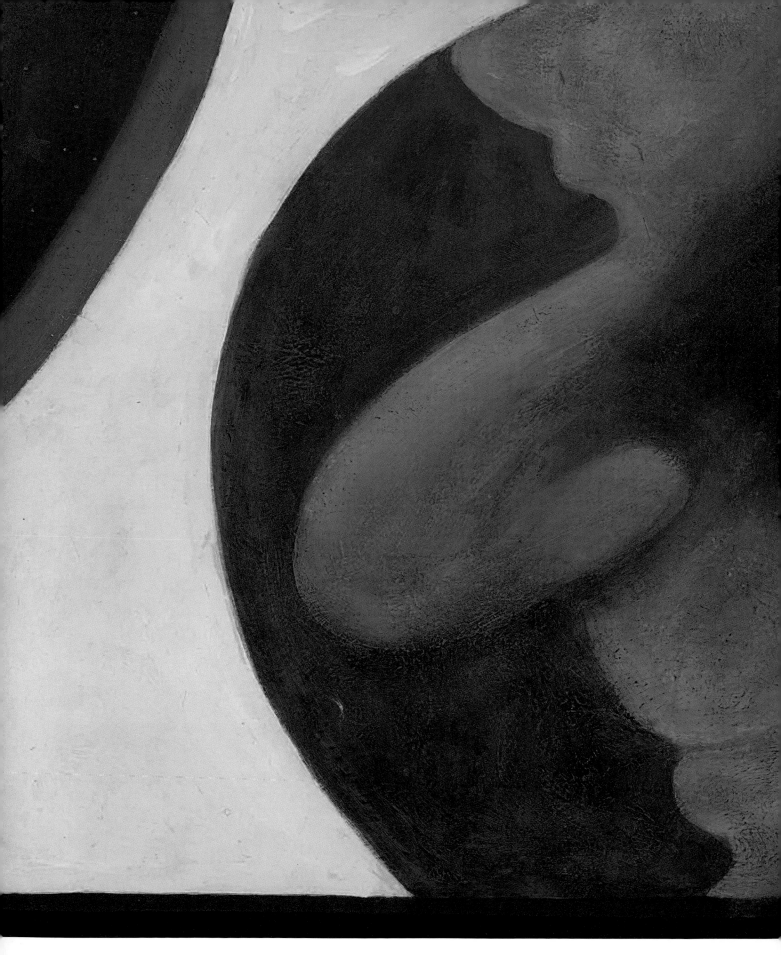

But my work backstage

begins much earlier.

I water the stars.

I erase the clouds

from the sky.

I paint the flowers.

I dress the birds

in long black coats.

I train wild dogs

to howl at the ◐ moon.

I suggest new glasses

for the owl.

I play tricky games

with the rats.

I feed the hungry

night monsters.

And I sprinkle star powder to give

the bears and dolls soft dreams.

Then I climb into the ◐ moon

for tonight's show.

It all began long, long ago,

and it starts anew every night.

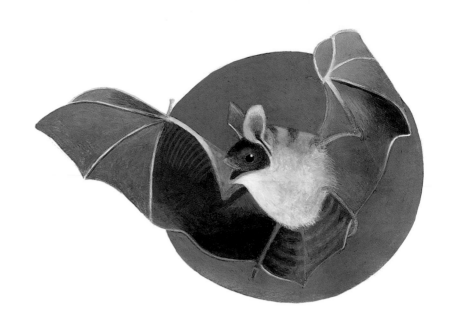

It's my ● moon theater.